SHOO WEE OKAPI

Written by Leslie McCrary

To you and your own two stinky feet

Leslie

ISBN 978-1-949522-05-1 Text copyright© 2018 by StoryBook Genius Publishing. Illustrations copyright© 2018 StoryBook Genius Publishing.

STORYBOOK
GENIUS PUBLISHING
sbgpublishing.com

Book
Design by
yipjar.com

SHOO WEE UKAPI!

Do you smell that?

Oh man, do I ever!

That is

funky.

You aren't kidding.

It smells like...like...

I know.

Let's take a really deep breath and...

Ohhhhhh! That smell! Well, um, yes. I know that smell.

It's, um, **my feet.**

Giraffe, oh gentle Giraffe, my only living relative, did you think this tar-like substance on my feet is all for the ladies? Scent de Shoo Wee perhaps?

Well, not exactly but...

SHOO WEE OKAPI Nº5

With feet like these, I'm hard to forget.
Everyone knows where I stand!

Okapi, just one question...

What do your friends
think about your feet?

Friends?

Yes, friends. Don't you have friends?

Hmmmmmm...not really. No one is a fan of my feet.
What?????? Well, no more feeling forgotten.
Let's fix your feet!

Fix my feet?

Yes! We can make them fragrant! It'll be fun!

I'm fine. I don't want all the fuss.

Okapi, I think you are really magical, stinky feet and all. Guess you're off to go lick your ears in some dark corner of the rainforest?

Yes sir! After all, they don't call me African Unicorn for nothing.

Giraffe, friends come and go.
But my stinky four feet are here to stay.
I mean, I'd much rather have four funky feet
than a truckload of elephant ear wax.
And have you ever smelled a
hippo's breath?

Eeeewww!

Exactly.
Not so different than
stinky feet, huh?

Fun Facts...

Scent glands on each foot of the okapi leave behind a tar-like, super stinky substance that communicates their territory.

Okapis are the only living relative of the giraffe.

Okapis can lick their own ears and wash their own eyelids.

Okapis are nearly impossible to observe in the wild and, once discovered, obtained a mythical reputation and gained the name "African unicorn."

CPSIA information can be obtained
at www.ICGtesting.com
Printed in the USA
LVHW072002220219
608476LV00015B/410/P

Okapis can lick their own ears and wash their own eyelids.

Okapis are nearly impossible to observe in the wild and, once discovered, obtained a mythical reputation and gained the name "African unicorn."

CPSIA information can be obtained
at www.ICGtesting.com
Printed in the USA
LVHW072002220219
608476LV00015B/410/P

9 781949 522051